Cell Pho...

published by

National Center for Youth Issues
ncyi.org
Practical Guidance Resources
Educators Can Trust

www.ncyi.org

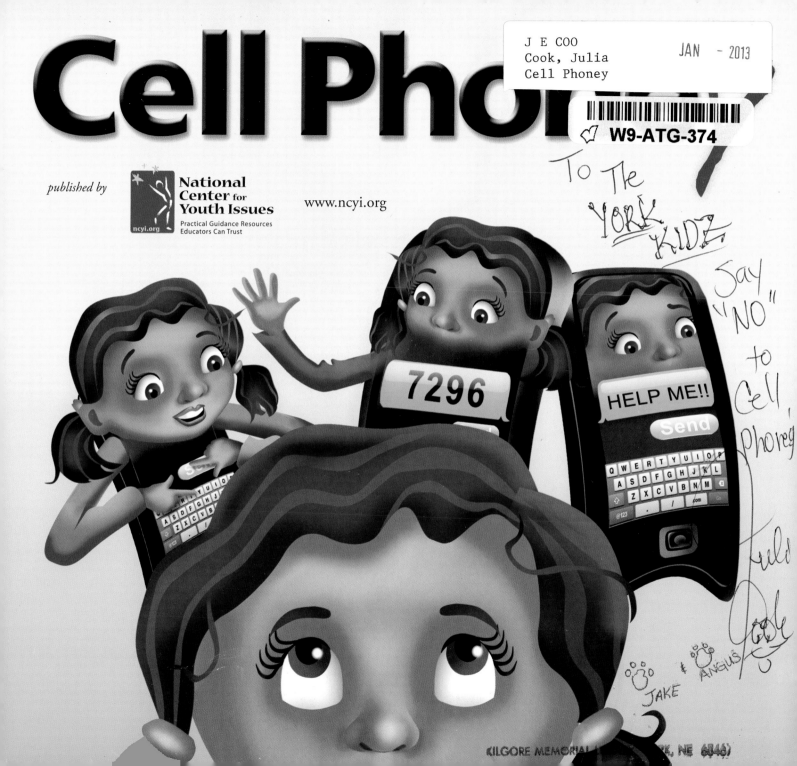

7296

HELP ME!!

Send

To The YORK KIDZ
Say "NO" to Cell Phoney

JAKE & ANGUS

To Robert... A man with great vision.
–Julia

Duplication and Copyright

**National
Center for
Youth Issues**
Practical Guidance Resources
Educators Can Trust
ncyi.org

P.O. Box 22185
Chattanooga, TN 37422-2185
423.899.5714 • 800.477.8277
fax: 423.899.4547
www.ncyi.org

ISBN: 978-1-937870-10-2
© 2012 National Center for Youth Issues, Chattanooga, TN
All rights reserved.

Written by: Julia Cook
Illustrations by: Anita DuFalla
Design by: Phillip W. Rodgers
Contributing Editor: Beth Spencer Rabon
Published by National Center for Youth Issues
Softcover

Printed at RR Donnelley • Reynosa, Tamaulipas, Mexico • November 2012

My name is Joanie Maloney, and I am the most excited person on the planet!

After years and years, and months and months, and days and days, I am finally getting my very own, brand new cell phone…well, it isn't exactly brand new. My mom got an upgrade and a new phone, so she is giving me her old phone.

Finally! I'll be able to text all of my friends whenever I want to!

I'll be able to download my music and listen to it whenever I want to!

I'll be able to call and talk to people whenever I want to!

I'll be able to surf the Net whenever I want to!

Now my life will be **PERFECT!**

www.coolshoesar

"Joanie, my mom said. Having your own cell phone is a big responsibility. It is also a privilege...not a right! Before I give you this phone, you have to attend my version of a *cell phone safety course*, so you will learn about the rules that go along with having your own cell phone."

"A *safety course*?...
Mom, it's a phone...
it's not a weapon!"

Cell Phone
Safety
Course

CONTRACT

"Yes, but if a cell phone is used incorrectly, it can hurt people, and the last thing I want is for this phone to totally consume you and take over your life!"

"Mom...it's *just* a cell phone!"

"Yes, but it won't be *your* cell phone unless you attend
the course, sign the contract, and follow the rules.

Now sit down, and let's get started!"

RULE #1

Never let your phone take over your life. Remember, your name is *Joanie*.

If your voice only comes through your cell phone,

then you'll become a *Cell Phoney!*

RULE #2

Never text or talk on your phone
while you're driving

your **feet**,

your **bike**,

and especially

your **car**.

Bad things can
happen that
can hurt **you**
and **others**,
and we like you
the way
that you are.

No text or talk can be more important than keeping my Joanie safe.

Your phone is not your oxygen source.

There's always a right time and place.

9

RULE #3

This phone is a good thing, and it should be used to help you in many ways.

Never use this phone to hurt others, or I'll just have to take it away.

Make sure that you don't text too much, even though texting might be your choice.

Some people forget how to talk to each other, and texting takes over their voice.

RULE #5

Make sure that your text messages pass the **"Grandma Test,"** each time before you hit .

If a grandma wouldn't like what you're texting, don't send it... instead, hit **End**.

RULE #6

Feel free to take pictures and send them to others, but make sure that your pictures are **clean**.

If it can't be displayed on a billboard, **it should *never* show up on your screen!**

"You might think this contract is a waste of your time, and you might think it's full of baloney.

But if you don't follow my cell phone rules, you'll turn into

Joanie Cell Phoney."

I rolled my eyes at my mom, signed the contract, grabbed my new phone and headed to my room.

AT LAST!!! My perfect life will now begin. I programmed in all of my friends' numbers and email addresses, sent out texts to everyone I could think of, and downloaded the coolest ring tone that I could find. Then, I plugged in my phone and went to sleep.

The next morning, I awoke to the amazing sound of my cell phone alarm playing my favorite song, and I started my perfect day.

My dad talked to me during breakfast, but I really didn't hear what he said.

I was too busy texting Martha. Her pink hair dye had turned her hair red.

Then while I was walking to school,
I downloaded a song that was free.

But I didn't watch where I was going,
and I walked right into a tree.

17

As soon as I got to my classroom, I saw Gerald picking his nose.

So, I whipped out my
phone to take pictures.

Because I
knew where
this would go!

I sent the video to everyone that I had contacts for in my phone.

I'm sure they will laugh when they see this, 'cause we all know that picking is

GROSS!

When my teacher called on me in Science,
I didn't know what to say next.

I hadn't heard her question,
'cause I was too busy sending a text.

It's hard not to check on an email,
especially when you know who it's from.

Who cares about Math and English?

My cell phone is **SO MUCH FUN**!

onecoolgirl@sbb.com

R U planning 2 go 2
the dance Friday?

C U

LOL

At lunch when I tried to order,
my words turned to numbers instead.

A cheeseburger, fries and a salad,
came out *"7 2 9 6 SEND."*

I'll have a 7296 SEND.

At the end of the day when I had to walk home, I could barely move my feet.

I was trapped inside of my cell phone, and I couldn't even tweet!

Send

When my mom saw my face, she started to cry, and she dropped our macaroni.

"Oh NO!" she said, with tears in her eyes...

My daughter's become a *Cell Phoney!*"

Suddenly, I heard my favorite song in the background...
the song I had chosen for my cell phone alarm.

It was all a dream...a dream that
felt like a nightmare, that is.

Wow, I guess cell phones really
are pretty powerful. I'm sure glad
that didn't happen in real life.

I unplugged my phone, turned it off, and threw it into my backpack.

Then, I headed downstairs to have breakfast and *talk* to my dad.

"Cell Phoney" Prevention Tips

Cell phones have drastically impacted the way people communicate. They offer almost unlimited access to the world in which we live. It is important to establish age-appropriate boundaries for your child when it comes to using a cell phone. Here are a few tips.

- Ask yourself, **"Does my child *need* a cell phone, or do they just *want* one?"**

- Make sure *you* set a good cell phone user example for your child. (You cannot expect your child not to text and drive if they see you doing it, etc.)

- **For younger children:** Avoid phones with texting or Instant Messaging (IM) capabilities. Program in all names and numbers that are important for your child to know. Discourage your child from answering a call from a number that he/she does not recognize. Thoroughly discuss how, when, and why the phone should be used.

- **For older children:** Reinforce how, when and why the phone should be used. Always expect your child to answer calls from you. Make sure the phone is turned off at night. Strongly discourage cell phone usage during meal time and other family times. Purchase the texting plan that works best for your family. Monitor your child's text messages, phone calls, and times of usage. Have your child review your cell phone bill with you. Discuss and strongly discourage cyberbullying, sexting, texting, talking while driving, and other inappropriate cell phone behaviors. Establish and enforce realistic consequences for improper cell phone usage.

- Remember the cell phone is *never* the cause of the problem…it's the person using the cell phone that causes the problem.

I flipped my phone to Video and started to film Gerald pick.

Then I watched as he rolled up a booger, and attempted the

"mighty flick."

20